Dizz
and the Talkie

Illustrations by Craig Cameron

EGMONT

95% of the paper used in this book is recycled paper, the remaining 5% is an Egmont grade 5 paper that comes from well-managed forests. For more information about Egmont's paper policy please visit www.egmont.co.uk/ethicalpublishing

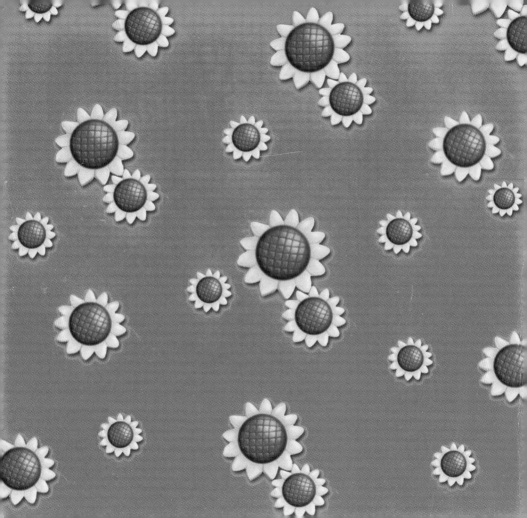

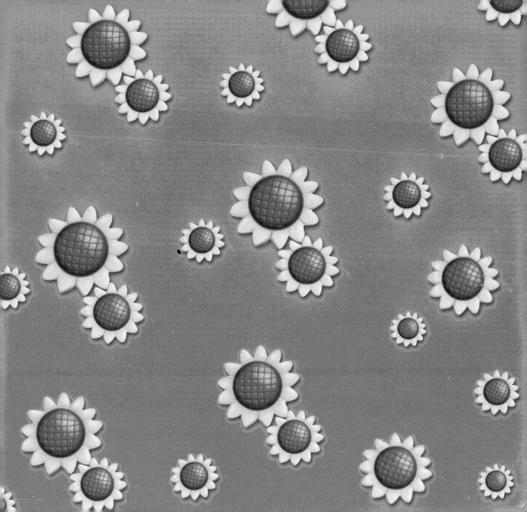

EGMONT

We bring stories to life

First published in Great Britain 2007
by Egmont UK Limited,
239 Kensington High Street, London W8 6SA

HiT entertainment

ISBN 978 1 4052 3143 5

3 5 7 9 10 8 6 4
Printed in Italy

FSC
Mixed Sources
Product group from well-managed
forests and other controlled sources
Cert no. TT-COC-002332
www.fsc.org
© 1996 Forest Stewardship Council

Egmont is passionate about helping to preserve the world's remaining ancient forests.
We only use paper from legal and sustainable forest sources.

This book is made from paper certified by the Forestry Stewardship Council (FSC),
an organisation dedicated to promoting responsible management of forest resources.
For more information on the FSC, please visit www.fsc.org. To learn more about
Egmont's sustainable paper policy, please visit www.egmont.co.uk/ethical

When Wendy brings the talkie-talkies to Sunflower Valley the machines have lots of fun with them. But Dizzy soon finds out how helpful they can be . . .

One sunny morning, Bob and the team were gathered around a large metal tank in the new yard in Sunflower Valley.

"This will be our new water tank," Bob told the machines. "We can use it to store our water. We will pump the water from the ground through the pipes using a hand pump."

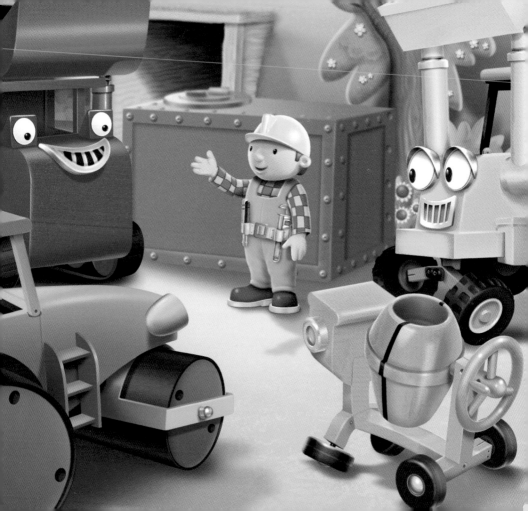

"Hello, everyone!" called Wendy driving in to the yard on Scrambler.

"I've got a present for each of you. They're called talkie-talkies! You can use the headsets to talk to each other wherever you are in Sunflower Valley!" said Wendy, as she handed out the headsets.

"Rock and roll!" smiled Roley.

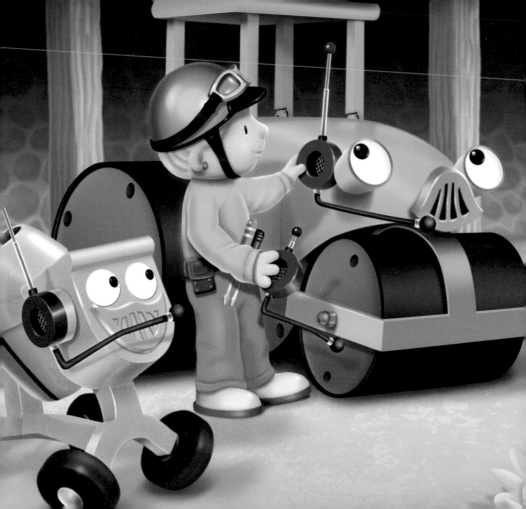

"That reminds me," said Bob. "We still need some rocks for the tank."

"Dizzy and I can go and find rocks," suggested Scrambler. "We can use the talkie-talkies to let Muck know when we find some. Let's scram!"

"Remember your way so you can get back," called Wendy, as they left.

"OK team? Can we build it?" Bob asked.

"Yes we can!" everyone cheered.

"Then let's get started! Lofty, you will be getting soil out using this special drill so we can reach the water."

"OK, Bob," said Lofty, and he got to work.

"Dizzy to Scrambler! Can you hear me?" asked Dizzy.

The friends were having fun using the talkie-talkies!

"Cor, look at that big boulder," said Scrambler. "We won't forget we passed that!"

Dizzy and Scrambler came to a sudden stop. There had been a landslide and the path was blocked with rocks!

Dizzy called Muck to tell him they had found some rocks. Muck set off down the track that Dizzy and Scrambler had taken.

Very soon, Muck came to the big boulder. "Muck to Dizzy, which way do I go at the big boulder, please?" he asked, using his talkie-talkie.

"Erm, you turn left," Dizzy told Muck.

Muck carried on until he came to two trees that looked like an arch. Dizzy couldn't remember seeing an arch. "Go right, I think," said Dizzy.

"And where do I go at the woods?" asked Muck.

"Erm, I don't remember any woods," replied Dizzy.

"Oh, no!" cried Muck. "I'm lost!"

Dizzy had an idea. "What can you see around you?" she asked Muck.

"Erm, a big hill with a cloud on top," replied Muck.

"Cool as a mule, Muck! Coz I see the big hill with the cloud, too," added Scrambler, over his talkie-talkie. "Head for the hill and you should find us."

Dizzy and Scrambler were starting to wonder if Muck would ever find them when Muck appeared suddenly.

"Muck's on the job!" he grinned. "Let's load up those rocks and get them back to Bob."

"But we don't know how to get back," moaned Scrambler.

Dizzy remembered how Muck had found them.

"Dizzy to Roley," she whispered into the talkie-talkie. "What big things can you see?"

"A really tall tree, taller than all the others," Roley whispered back.

"Come on!" Dizzy told Roley and Muck. "Let's head for the really tall tree!"

Back at the yard, Bob was beginning to wonder where Dizzy, Scrambler and Muck had got to.

"Call them on the talkie-talkie base unit!" suggested Wendy.

"Bob to Dizzy!" Bob began.

"Dizzy to Bob!" came a voice right behind him. "We're back! And we've got rocks."

Soon the water tank was finished. Wendy tried the pump and the pipes began to rattle.

Splash! Water flew out of the pipes and soaked poor Bob!

"Dizzy to Bob," giggled Dizzy. "Hee, hee, you left the tap on!"

"Oh, Dizzy!" said Bob. And everybody began to laugh! It was another job well done for Bob and the machine team.

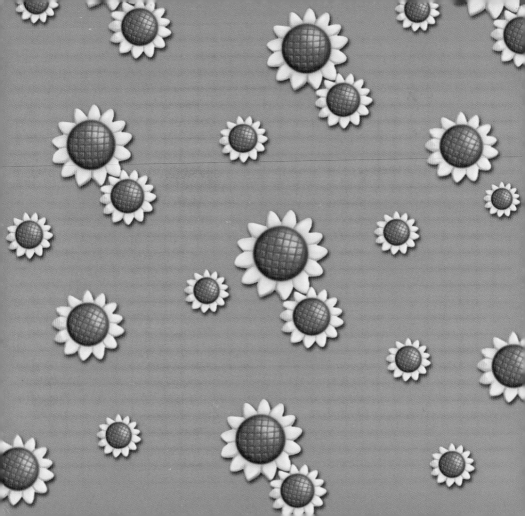

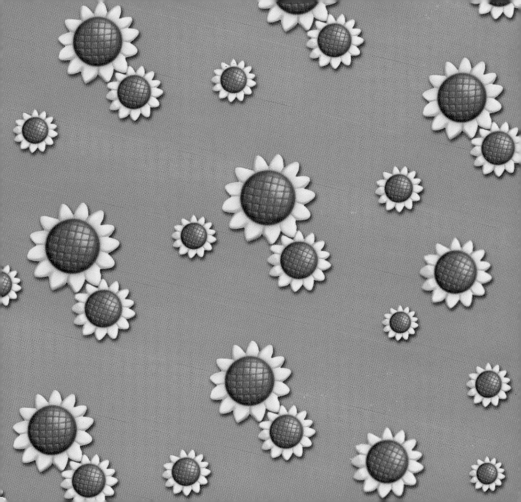

Start collecting your Bob the Builder Story Library NOW!

1. Bob and the Big Plan
2. Dizzy and the Talkie-Talkie
3. Scrambler and the Off-road Race
4. Wendy and the Surprise Party
5. Roley and the Woodland Walk
6. Benny and the Important Job
7. Sumsy and the Sunflower Spill
8. Muck and the Machine Convoy
9. Travis and the Tropical Fruit
10. Lofty and the Singing Stars
11. Scoop and the Bakery Build
12. Spud and the Funny Trees
13. Packer and the Difficult Day
14. Dodger and the Dairy Delivery
15. Pilchard and the Big Surprise
16. Tumbler and the Skate Park
17. Gripper, Grabber and the Sports Stadium
18. Scruffty and the Goat Hunt
19. Flex and the Fix-it Day
20. Bristle and the Big Clean

1 BOB TOKEN · 1 BOB TOKEN · BOB

'Bob Goodies Please' Reply Card

Yes I have enclosed 4 special Bob Tokens so please send me a FREE Bob the Builder poster and door hanger ☐ (tick here)

Simply fill in your details below and send this page to:
BOB OFFERS, PO BOX 715, HORSHAM RH12 5WG

To be completed by an adult

Fan's name:
....

Address:
....

....

.... **Postcode:**
....

Email:
....

Date of birth:

Name of parent / guardian:

Signature of parent / guardian:

Bob the Builder

Ref: BOB 006